ALL OF MY EMOTIONS

Written By
Britney Wilson-Penny

Illustrated By
Sanghamitra Dasgupta

Acknowledgments:

To my family and friends who supported my book, thank you for showing love. To my love Dorian, thank you for supporting me and ALWAYS believing in me even when I don't believe in myself. I love you. Special thanks to my good friend Rasheeda Seawell for helping me put all my ideas together and for guiding me in the right direction with the book. I really appreciate you.

DEDICATION

This book is dedicated to my children De'Yanna Alston, Braylen Alston, and Cree Alston. I've failed at many things in life but the one thing I've never failed at is being your mother. Thanks for helping me grow into the woman I am today. I Love You!

I am surprised

I am scared

I am nervous

   **I**

   **am**

   **me**

Draw how you are feeling and write it down

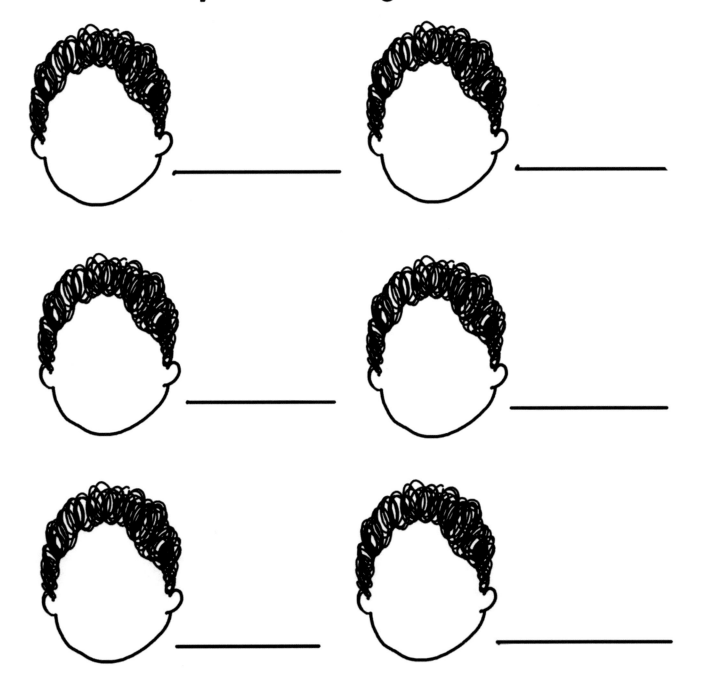

Match the word with the picture emotion

1. Afraid

2. Angry

3. Happy

4. Sad

Finish the face

Draw the Correct emotion to match the word

1. Anger   _____

2. Sorrow   _____

3. Happy   _____

4. Joy   _____

5. Excitement   _____

6. Terrified   _____

How Are You Feeling Today?

B	T	Z	R	A	N	G	R	Y	G
O	K	L	T	H	R	Q	N	M	L
E	X	C	I	T	E	D	A	T	A
H	S	U	R	P	R	I	S	E	D
D	B	C	E	R	A	F	H	K	G
S	V	A	D	O	N	E	Y	O	J
A	C	L	A	U	H	A	P	P	Y
D	X	M	B	D	K	L	Z	S	W

draw a picture of how you're feel today

ABOUT THE AUTHOR

My name is Britney Wilson-Penny. I have been working with children for over fourteen years. "I believe the children are our future." Each child is capable of bringing something unique to this world. As an educator I would want to share my own love and passion for learning with children.